PUFFIN BOOKS

Jumble

Kathryn Cave is the author of *Dragonrise* and many other books for children of all ages. She studied Philosophy at Oxford and then at the Massachusetts Institute of Technology. Both as a girl and as an adult she spent long periods in America and has also lived in Australia. She was a freelance editor before she turned to writing. Kathyrn Cave lives in West London and is married with three children.

Jumble

Kathryn Cave

Illustrated by Chris Riddell

and

Andrew Takes
the Plunge

Illustrated by David Mostyn

PUFFIN BOOKS

PUFFIN BOOKS

Published by the Penguin Group
Penguin Books Ltd, 27 Wrights Lane, London W8 5TZ, England
Penguin Books USA Inc., 375 Hudson Street, New York, New York 10014, USA
Penguin Books Australia Ltd, Ringwood, Victoria, Australia
Penguin Books Canada Ltd, 10 Alcorn Avenue, Toronto, Ontario, Canada M4V 3B2
Penguin Books (NZ) Ltd, 182–190 Wairau Road, Auckland 10, New Zealand

Penguin Books Ltd, Registered Offices: Harmondsworth, Middlesex, England

· *Jumble* first published by Blackie Children's Books 1991
Andrew Takes the Plunge first published by Blackie Children's Books 1994
Published together in Puffin Books 1995
1 3 5 7 9 10 8 6 4 2

Text copyright © Kathryn Cave, 1991, 1994
Illustrations copyright © Chris Riddell, 1991 and
© David Mostyn, 1994
All rights reserved

The moral right of the author has been asserted

Filmset in Plantin

Made and printed in Great Britain by Clays Ltd, St Ives plc

Jumble

For Eleanor, Joseph and Alice

Chapter One

Andrew was hopeless about jumble sales. He'd buy anything, anything at all.

'Can I have a pound of my pocket money early?' he asked one Saturday at breakfast. Everyone knew what it meant.

'Don't let him have it, Mum,' said Andrew's sister Lynne. 'You know what'll happen. You know what he's like.' It was none of her business, but that never stopped Lynne.

'Go on, Mum,' pleaded Andrew.

'Ah well . . .' Andrew's mother sighed

and reached for her handbag. 'It's for a good cause. Only try and be sensible this time, love. Don't buy anything you can't carry home. No more wardrobes for 40p.'

'No more chairs with their insides hanging out,' chimed in Lynne. 'No more three-legged tables.'

'No furniture really, dear. We've got enough.'

'No more stag's heads with broken antlers,' Lynne went on from deep in her magazine. 'No stuffed gorillas.'

'I wouldn't buy a stuffed gorilla,' said Andrew, stung. 'I'm not stupid am I? Where would I put it? Where would it go?'

'Don't ask me,' said Lynne. 'You're the one who brings home mouldy alligators—'

'Only one. And it's not mouldy and it's not an alligator. It's a crocodile.'

'—and leaves them lying on the landing to ladder people's tights. I'm fed up with having to climb over it to get to the bathroom. Why don't you put it in your own room, for crying out loud?'

'Don't be daft, Lynne,' said Andrew's brother Rob. 'There's no space in Andrew's room, is there?'

'Well, not a lot,' Andrew admitted cautiously.

'Of course not,' Rob agreed. '*His* room's full of valuable antiques: broken tennis rackets, stuff like that.'

'I'm mending that racket. I *told* you.'

'Fishing nets with holes that'd let a shark through. Worth a fortune. Think of it, Lynne: the chances are there are only two hand-held whaling nets in the world and our little brother's got both of them. Not to mention a priceless three-legged table.'

'There were four legs when I bought it, I know there were.' Andrew was getting flustered. 'One must have fallen off. Or someone took it.'

'Well, don't look at me.' Rob gave a hollow laugh. 'I'm the mug who's spent the last three months trying to mend it for you. Every time I drill a hole in it something falls off. It's got woodworm, Andrew, and dry rot, and death-watch beetle too, I wouldn't be surprised. What

9

did you want to go and buy a table like that for anyway?'

'They're useful, tables,' Andrew explained. You'd think Rob and Lynne were thick sometimes. He hunted for the right words. 'You can put things on them.'

Lynne turned to Rob and shook her head. 'Don't talk to him. It's not worth it. You might as well talk to that alligator.'

'Crocodile,' said Andrew distinctly.

'You ought to get it off the landing, whatever it is. It's dangerous.' Lynne put down one magazine and reached for another from the box by the sofa. 'There'll be an accident one day.' She flicked open the magazine. A cloud of dust like ancient pepper rose from the pages. 'Good grief, Andrew. Where did these magazines come from? This one's

twenty-three years old. I'm going to need
a gas mask to read it.'

'I'll keep my eye open for one,' said
Andrew, always glad to help. 'I'll be off
then.'

He was half-way to the door when there
came a rumbling crashing thudding
bump-bump-bump that started somewhere upstairs and ended outside the
door to the hall. Andrew's mother got up

from the table clucking with alarm.

'There! It's happened,' said Lynne without looking up. 'I knew it would. And I bet you whatever it is, it turns out to be *his* fault.'

Andrew was about to say something crushing when the door from the hall opened. 'Dad!' he said instead. 'Are you all right?' He was the sort of boy who noticed things and he couldn't help feel-

ing something was wrong.

'Do I look all right?' said his father. 'Because if I do, it's a miracle. What I ought to look like is someone who's tripped over a stuffed alligator and fallen down fourteen stairs, bouncing off the banister three times on the way. I think I've got the numbers right. Do you want to say anything, Andrew, before I go on?'

'It's a crocodile, Dad. I keep *telling* people. Oh no!' A terrible thought struck Andrew. 'You didn't tread on it did you?'

'Right,' said Andrew's dad. 'That does it. Listen to me, Andrew, and listen well. I don't care what that animal is or was. It can be a polar bear for all I care. Get it off the landing before lunch or I'll do worse than tread on it. And start now. Yes, this minute. Do you hear me?'

'Now?' said Andrew, stretching his brain to its limits. 'You mean right away?'

His father nodded grimly. 'But what about the jumble sale?'

'Give me strength,' said Andrew's dad to nobody in particular. 'I've had it up to here with you and jumble sales. I want that landing clear by the time we've done the shopping. Someone will have to stay behind with you. Lynne, it's your turn.'

Lynne was not pleased. In the end she said, 'All right. I suppose I could have a bath and try that new face stuff. Just tell him he's not to pester me, that's all.'

Andrew's father told him not to pester Lynne. He said a lot of other things Andrew thought were uncalled for. 'And see to the rest of your junk too,' he finished, waving a hand around. 'There's no room to swing a cat in here.'

'We don't have a cat,' Andrew pointed out.

Nobody listened.

'It's high time you had a clear-up, love,' said Andrew's mum, tucking a shopping list into her handbag. 'There'll be other sales. Keep the pound till then. See you later.' She wriggled out of the chair with its insides hanging out and headed for the door.

Andrew's father plucked his cap from the stag's antlers. 'You coming with us, Robert? Get your coat then. The car-park will be filling up. No, Andrew, not another word. Sort this lot out and then talk to me about jumble sales.' The door shut.

'It's time you grew up, Andrew,' Lynne said, abandoning her magazine with a yawn. 'I'm having the bathroom for the next two hours, OK? And in case you were thinking of moving that alligator into my room, don't.' She left.

'Nor mine,' said Rob. 'In fact do something about that table while you're upstairs. You wouldn't believe the noise those woodworm make. I hardly had a wink of sleep last night. Cheerio, Andrew.'

Andrew ran to the front door. 'If I get all that done – the table, the back room, the crocodile and everything – can I go to the jumble sale then?' he shouted up the front path.

'I can't hear you,' his dad shouted, quickly rolling up the car window. His mother smiled and waved. The car drove off.

'That means yes,' said Andrew, cheering up immediately. 'Right. I'll get started. Shouldn't take me long. Half an hour at the most.' He shut the door and bounded up the stairs whistling.

Chapter Two

Andrew's crocodile was broad and squat, 189 centimetres from snout to tail. It had wicked black eyes and a fearsome snarl slightly spoiled by lack of teeth. You'd notice a crocodile like that anywhere – that was one of the things Andrew loved about it. You certainly noticed it on the landing.

Andrew ran his hand over the crocodile's polished scales and frowned. There was a dent that hadn't been there last time he looked. And a dollop of white stuff on its nose: toothpaste? Shaving cream?

Andrew dabbed at it and sniffed his finger: shaving cream. Rob! That settled it: the landing was no place for a crocodile. With some difficulty Andrew hoisted one end off the carpet and hauled it towards his bedroom.

The bedroom door was open. It had to be: the room was so full, it wouldn't shut. To get in or out Andrew had to squeeze between a small statue of King Richard the Lionheart and a crate of non-matching crockery. The crocodile complicated things.

When he was in at last, Andrew paused to get his breath back and take stock of the situation.

It didn't take long. The situation was roughly this.

The shelves were full. The chest of

drawers was full. The floor was full. You didn't have to look under the bed to know it was full too. Even the air was full, with models hanging on strings from the ceiling.

It was a nice room, lived-in, but there was no obvious place for a crocodile.

Andrew looked at the ceiling. He had a feeling there was a coil of rope in the garage. If he used that, and moved the

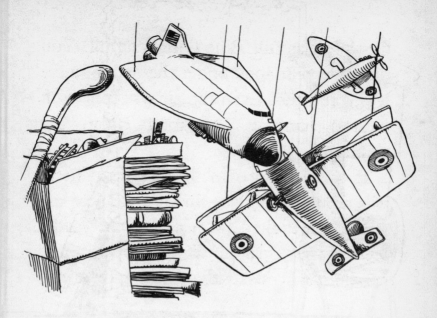

space shuttle and the Sopwith Camel from above the bed to beside the window . . .? That would make room for the crocodile. What if it fell though? Andrew was used to the models falling down, but they were light. The crocodile wasn't. If it landed on you, you'd know you'd been landed on. If you lived to tell the tale, that is. No, there had to be another way.

Staring round the room in desperation,

Andrew's eye eventually came to the cupboard. It was shut – and the door taped up with sticky tape too, Andrew could see. He couldn't remember why he'd stuck the tape on, or when the cupboard was last open. He thought it must have been a long time ago. There might be space to squeeze a crocodile inside, there just might.

Andrew edged his way round the boxes where his jigsaw puzzle collection was being sorted, did a sort of hop over something he'd bought thinking it was a record-player only to discover it wasn't, and ended up within striking distance of the cupboard door. A mere five minutes later, he scratched off the last strip of tape with the crocodile's tail and pressed down the catch.

The door flew open.

Suddenly it came back to Andrew why

he'd kept the cupboard shut for the past six months. It was full too – more than full. Bursting. With the door open it could burst at last.

'Oh no!' cried Andrew.

There was a rumble like an avalanche about to slide.

'Blimey. Lynne, somebody, help!'

But Lynne was in the bathroom with both taps running and the door locked. Andrew was on his own. He hugged the crocodile close and waited for the storm to break.

It was quite an avalanche. In the early stages Andrew recognised a cracked cricket bat, a stringless tennis racket, a tin of marbles, three football boots, a music stand, a frogman's suit and the whaling nets. Then a roller-skate hit him on the head and he lost track.

'Well,' he said when he opened his eyes

again. 'There's room in the cupboard now. I'll put the crocodile in first. I can clear up later.'

The problem was to get to the cupboard.

First Andrew trod on the marbles. Then he got his foot stuck in the tennis racket. While he was still trying to kick it free, the whaling nets turned into crocodile nets.

'What the—?' Andrew said the first time the crocodile's tail got stuck. 'Useless nets,' he said the fourth. Still, he kicked and slid and stumbled and staggered his way through the rest of the wreckage to reach the cupboard.

'Thank goodness that's over,' he said when he got there. But it wasn't over yet.

He tried putting the crocodile in snout first. The tail stuck out.

He tried to get the crocodile out again.

It wouldn't come.

He gritted his teeth and heaved with all his strength. The crocodile flew out and landed on top of Andrew, along with the clothes rail, two sweaters and a pair of jeans.

When Andrew was on his feet again, he tried putting the crocodile in tail first. That didn't work any better.

The truth was, lengthways, sideways, diagonally, right way up or upside down – it didn't matter how Andrew tried it. The crocodile was *bigger* than the cupboard. There was always something – a paw or a jaw or a claw – that wouldn't fit.

The only way to get the crocodile into the cupboard would be to saw it in half.

'Useless cupboard,' said Andrew.

As he hauled the crocodile out for the tenth time its tail went out of control and

swiped the books off the shelf above the bed. The *Boy's Own Annual* for 1957 landed on Andrew's head.

When he came to, he was lying on the bed with the crocodile on his chest. 'Right,' he said. 'That's it. Dad's got a point. I do have too much stuff. Something's got to go.'

Something seemed to be wrong with his sight. Were there two crocodiles all along? Andrew crossed and uncrossed his eyes vigorously. To his relief the second crocodile disappeared.

Andrew sat up, feeling rather light-headed. 'I *will* have a good clear-out,' he told the remaining crocodile. 'I'll have the best clear-out ever. I'll get rid of all the stuff nobody wants *and* I'll get to the jumble sale. I know what to do at last.'

Chapter Three

'Yes,' Andrew was saying into the telephone five minutes later. '11 Upton Road. Turn left at the pool. That's right. You'll need a car to collect it though. A big car. Well, maybe a van. Do you have a lorry?'

'Oh yes,' he said again. 'It's quite all right. My parents know all about it. No, I'm not on my own. My big sister's here.'

'In half an hour?' he said at last. 'Yes. I'll have everything ready. On the pavement outside the house. Oh, it's nothing.

33

It's in a good cause, isn't it? No, thank *you*. Goodbye.'

Andrew hung up the phone delighted. Half an hour? Time to get cracking.

'Here – what's going on over the road?' said Mr Turnbull from number 16.

'What do you mean?' asked Mrs Turnbull.

'There's a stag's head on the pavement. Look!'

His wife looked. 'Probably having a party.'

'Funny party. And there's something else – is it a chair or what?'

The chair with its insides out was upside-down by the stag's head. It looked less like a chair than ever. 'Or what,' said Mrs Turnbull doubtfully.

'What's he bringing out now?' Mr Turnbull wiped the glass with his sleeve. 'Wrapped up in a sheet like that . . .

What do you reckon it is?'

Mrs Turnbull didn't hesitate. 'A body,' she said. 'Move over. Let's see who it is.'

Andrew emptied the bundle out onto the chair: books, magazines, tennis racket, football boots, crocodile nets, sweaters. No body.

Mrs Turnbull went away disappointed. 'He's got a pillowcase now,' was the next report. Mrs Turnbull sniffed. You couldn't get a body in there. 'He's got just about everything else in,' said Mr Turnbull.

Roller-skates, marbles, jigsaw puzzles, an ancient set of encyclopaedias tumbled out onto the mound on the pavement. Andrew mopped his brow with the pillowcase and disappeared.

'Well, that must be everything,' Mr Turnbull said ten minutes later.

The mound was the size of a small

mountain. Passers-by had to cross the road to avoid it.

'He's lowered out the big stuff from the front bedroom on a rope of knotted sheets.' Mr Turnbull pointed out the statue of Richard the Lionheart guarding the three-legged table with his sword. 'He's down to the small stuff now.'

Andrew tipped an assortment of small items off a battered tray onto the mountain's foothills. As he lobbed the tray up onto a peak, a white van pulled up.

'Oh blimey,' said Mr Turnbull, rubbing his hands. 'I'll have that cup of tea now. I'm going to enjoy this. They'll never get that lot in there, never.'

But they did. At ten minutes to eleven Andrew waved at Mr and Mrs Turnbull and squeezed into the back of the van beside Richard the Lionheart. The van drove off.

'Nothing more going to happen this morning,' said Mr Turnbull sadly. 'Might as well do the shopping.'

Once again Mr Turnbull was wrong. A lot more happened that morning.

At half-past eleven a white van pulled up outside number 11 Upton Road again. The driver jumped out and opened the doors at the back.

'Here we are,' he said. 'Door-to-door service. No charge. And considering what you've got there, I think it's only fair. We ought to pay you, I reckon.'

Andrew's head poked out of the back of the van. 'You couldn't give me a hand with it?' he asked anxiously. 'It could be a bit difficult.'

The driver thought. 'OK. We'd better cover it with that old blanket first though. Wouldn't want to give someone a heart attack.'

Andrew covered it up with a blanket. He and the driver carried it up the path.

'What next?' the driver asked while Andrew unlocked the front door.

'Not far,' Andrew told him. 'In through the door, along the hall, up the stairs, down the landing, and into my bedroom. That's all. It'll be easy.' He had his fingers crossed when he said the last bit.

Ten minutes later they made it through

the front door. 'Can't we leave it here?'
the driver asked.

'No,' said Andrew. 'We use this door.'

'What about here then?' the driver
asked half-way up the stairs.

'No – we've only got the one staircase.
It's not far now, I promise.'

'Here,' said the driver firmly when they
reached the bathroom door on the landing. 'The perfect place. Made for it.'

'No,' said Andrew with regret. 'Lynne's in the bathroom. She'd never get out again, would she?'

'You could feed her through the key-hole. Or under the door.' But Andrew still said no.

Andrew's bedroom door was open because he was used to it like that. They got the thing in a blanket in somehow,

although neither of them could ever say how.

'I won't stay, thank you,' the driver said when Andrew offered him a cup of tea. 'I've got a thing about crocodiles. And those too.' He pointed at the thing in a blanket. 'You won't get *that* out of here in a hurry, that's for sure.'

Andrew smiled and reached for the blanket. The driver turned hastily away.

'No,' Andrew said softly, 'I won't.'

Chapter Four

A quarter of an hour later Andrew's parents' car drove up. Andrew went down to help carry in the shopping. He didn't say anything about what he'd been doing. He wanted his clear-up to be a surprise.

It was.

When the shopping was stowed away Andrew's dad opened the door to the back room and tossed his cap in the general direction of the stag's antlers. 'Thank goodness that's done,' he said.

The cap fell on the carpet.

Andrew's dad blinked. He stared at the cap. He stared at the wall. No stag's head. No antlers. He was surprised all right. He looked as if he'd turned to stone.

Andrew's mum bustled in and made a beeline for the chair with its insides hanging out. She reached the corner where it ought to be. She stopped dead. She looked round the room. 'Who's moved the chair?' she said.

Andrew beamed. The surprise was working.

'It's gone!' she said. 'Gone!' She couldn't have sounded more surprised if the house had gone too.

'Hey!' There was a shout from upstairs. Rob's feet pounded down the staircase. 'Who's been in my room, eh? Where's that table I was mending?'

Andrew chortled. It only needed

Lynne to come down to make the surprise perfect.

The hall door opened and Lynne drifted in. 'What's all the fuss?' she asked as she sat down on the sofa and reached for the box of magazines. She reached this way and that way. She stood up and looked behind the sofa. She crouched down and peered underneath.

'All right!' said Lynne grimly. 'Where's my magazine?'

Everyone looked at Andrew. This was his moment.

'It's gone!' he said proudly. 'All the rubbish – the stag's head, the magazines, the table, everything. I cleared it out and I took it to a jumble sale. What do you think of that?'

They thought of that for perhaps ten seconds. Then everyone spoke at once.

'You moron,' said Rob. 'I've done a lot of work on that table.'

'It's the only chair for my bad back,' said Andrew's mum. 'It was just as I liked it.'

'You'd no right,' said Lynne. 'I was reading that magazine.'

'As if I hadn't enough to do,' said Andrew's dad, picking his cap off the floor. 'Which hall was it then? Speak up, Andrew. St Matthew's? Right! We'll have to get moving or it'll have finished.'

'What will have finished?' asked Andrew, reeling.

'The sale of course. And I'll have a word or two to say to you later, Andrew.' The door to the hall opened and shut with a bang.

'Wait for me,' said Lynne. She gave Andrew the sort of look that kills at twenty paces. 'Honestly!' she said in the sort of voice that goes with it.

'I'm coming too,' said Rob. 'As for you,' he said to Andrew, 'you thick brainless stupid ungrateful little twerp, words fail me.' He followed Lynne.

'What have I done?' asked Andrew, stunned.

His mum pressed her lips together and shook her head. 'I'll get the wheelbarrow,' she called to Rob and Lynne from the hall. 'We'll need something to wheel it back in. It won't fit in the car.'

'Wheel *what* back? *What* won't fit in the car?' asked Andrew in vain. The house was empty.

'Let me know what's going on some day, won't you?' he shouted down the street after them. 'Next year maybe. Or the year after.' But they were round the corner where sarcasm couldn't reach them. He shut the front door and went upstairs, seriously disgruntled.

An hour later strange sounds were to be heard from the side alley. After a few minutes someone banged on the back door. Andrew went down to see who it was.

'Yes?' he said in mild surprise. It's not every day you open the door to a walking stag's head.

'Out the way,' it said without moving its lips.

Andrew got out of the way smartish
and the stag's head came in, closely followed by Andrew's dad.

'Give us a hand then,' said his dad. 'I
can't do it all on my own. Over to the
wall. Now lift. Higher. Now go right.
There!' He stood back and beamed at the
stag's head, back in its old place on the
wall. When he turned to Andrew, the
beam faded. 'Lucky it hadn't gone, I
reckon,' he said severely.

He went over to the table and plonked down a bag.

'What's that?' asked Andrew.

'Just something that took my fancy.'

Andrew reached into the bag and then wished he hadn't. 'What sort of something?' he asked.

'Get it out and see.'

Gingerly Andrew got it out and put it on the table.

'Other way up, stupid.' Andrew's dad picked the something up and turned it over. 'There!'

'Is it a bird?' asked Andrew, interested. 'I thought birds had to have feathers. Why's it only got one eye, Dad?'

His father ignored the question. 'A bird! It's an Amazonian parrot, anyone can see that. Look at that expression. Marvellous. It's seen a thing or two, it has.'

'Not recently,' said Andrew, but his dad had darted away to adjust the stag's antlers. 'Hey!' There was a scraping and banging in the side alley. 'What's that?'

'Give me a hand then,' said Rob's voice.

Andrew went to the back door. 'That's that old table!' he cried. 'What did you bring that back for? It's only got two legs now! I thought you said it had woodworm.'

'It shows it's real wood, doesn't it?' said Rob scathingly. 'None of your plastic laminates. And they'd thrown away the third leg. I ask you! Throwing away something like that. You ought to be more careful what you go giving away, Andrew. Come on, help me get it up the stairs on its side.'

Andrew helped. 'What've you got on your head?' he asked when they'd got the

table into the bedroom. He thought it might be a dead ferret.

'Something I picked up,' said Rob.

'I'll put it in the bin, shall I?' Andrew looked round for a piece of newspaper to wrap it up in.

'The bin? Good grief, Andrew, that's real wool.' Rob took the dead ferret off and put it carefully on the table. 'A quality hat, that's what you're looking at.'

'Oh,' said Andrew.

'Not like the modern rubbish you get in the shops.'

'No.' Andrew paused, hunting for the right words. 'It's got a funny smell, hasn't it?'

'Needs airing, that's all.' Rob picked the quality hat up and thumped it briskly against the nearest bit of table. This happened to be a leg, which immediately

fell off. The smell of dead ferret and damp wood flowered like ripe cheese.

Andrew sensed it was time to go.

Downstairs he met Lynne dragging a tea-chest through the back door. 'Give us a hand,' she said. 'They're heavy, these magazines. Goodness knows where the one I want is. And I'll have lost my place too. Here, hold these while I look.'

Suddenly Andrew found himself clasping a prehistoric *Blue Peter Annual*, a purple handbag with a broken strap, and a knitted snake.

'Did you buy these?' It was possible she wasn't mad. Someone might have paid her to take them away.

'Of course I bought them,' said Lynne impatiently. 'You know what, Andrew? Sometimes you're really stupid. Oh, give them to me. Can't you hear Mum needs help?'

'Thank you, love,' said Andrew's mum as he helped her haul the chair out of the barrow. Its insides weren't hanging out any more – they'd vanished. 'Over in the corner, that's right. Ah, that's nice. That's lovely. And I picked up this while I was there.'

Andrew's mum pointed to what

Andrew had taken for a bit of rag. 'Unusual, isn't it? Make a lovely cushion. Holes? What holes? Oh *those* holes. All they need is a few patches. Right, Andrew, if you've stopped playing the fool, you go and pop the kettle on. We need a spot of tea before lunch.'

Andrew went.

After lunch everyone was back to normal.

Andrew's mum winked across the table at Andrew's dad. 'Didn't you buy anything at the sale yourself, love?' she asked Andrew. Andrew's dad winked back. 'You did? Let's see then.'

'It's upstairs,' said Andrew, bashful.

'Let's have a look,' said Rob.

'I'm coming too,' said Lynne, putting down her magazine.

They trooped upstairs. Andrew opened the door of his bedroom.

There was a stunned silence. Then: 'Oh dear, oh *dear*,' they said joyfully. 'You've really done it this time. Blimey, Andrew, you get worse each week. What *are* we going to do with *that*?'

Andrew Takes the Plunge

For Tamsin, Frances and Nicholas

Chapter One

Andrew was tall and skinny.

He liked jumble sales, football, reading and making plastic models.

He hated swimming.

He couldn't swim. He never went swimming. No one tried to make him.

Life was good.

And then one Monday, Mr Elliot, Andrew's teacher, stuck a notice up on the classroom window. The heading was in big black letters:

CAN YOUR CHILD SWIM?

Then came a lot of writing that Andrew didn't read because he had better things to do and he could see it was really boring. At the bottom was the telephone number of a local pool that gave swimming lessons.

When Andrew's mother rolled up to meet him after school, she saw the notice. Andrew goggled as she got out a pen and started jotting down details on the back of her cheque-book. When he asked why, she gave an encouraging smile that sent shivers all down his spine.

'It's high time you learned to swim, Andrew. I meant to sign you up for lessons years ago. Come on – Lynne'll be home first if we don't get a move on.'

As she towed him towards the gate, Andrew said, 'But Mum, I don't want swimming lessons. I hate swimming.'

She gave that smile again.

'Don't fret, love. We'll talk about it when we get home.'

In the car, Andrew hoped that by the time they got home she'd have forgotten about it. She did forget things.

She'd forgotten his dinner money only that morning.

Almost every Thursday he got to school and discovered she'd forgotten to tell him to bring his football boots (Mr Elliot kept a spare pair in his desk, specially for Andrew).

She also forgot to retrieve the old socks he stuffed under his bed because he was too busy to put them in the dirty-washing basket.

In Andrew's opinion, his mother was a talented all-round forgetter. But she didn't forget the swimming lessons.

'Mum, I hate swimming,' he said as soon as they got home. He spoke very slowly and clearly to make sure she understood.

'You don't hate it,' she said. Just like that. And while he was still reeling, she

added, 'You can't say you hate something when you don't even know how
to do it.'

'Andrew can,' Lynne said from the
sofa. She was fourteen and completely
different from Andrew – for example,
she played netball and sometimes
wore her hair in a pony-tail. You
wouldn't catch Andrew doing things
like that. Still, he thought, at least
she understood.

'I do hate swimming, Mum,' he said. 'I
really, really hate it. OK?'

It wasn't.

'Swimming's important,' his mother
said, looking stubborn. 'It could make a
big difference to you one day.'

'Oh yes?' Andrew was beginning to
get cross.

'Yes. And don't keep saying you hate

it. You might love it when you learn how.'

'I'll never learn,' Andrew said.

His mother acted as if she hadn't heard him. 'So I'll give them a ring about lessons tomorrow.' With that she marched out into the garden.

'What does she mean,' Andrew complained indignantly, 'saying swimming's important? I mean, look at *me*. I can't swim and it's never done me any harm at all. I *like* not being able to swim.'

'Your liking it is irrelevant,' Lynne said loftily. While Andrew was trying to work out if that was an insult, she went on: 'And anyway, you might not always like not being able to swim.'

Yet another way in which Lynne was completely different from him was the

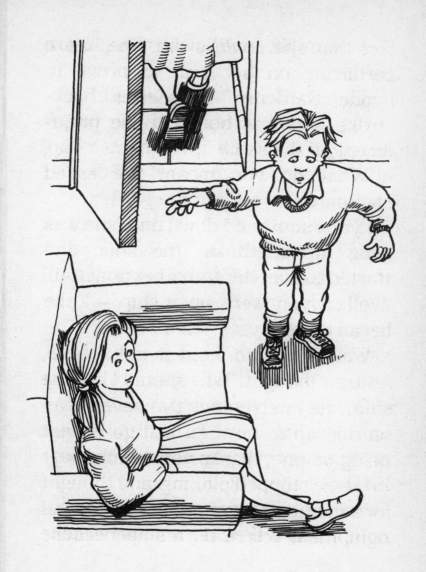

fact that she *could* swim. She had a certificate on her wall to prove it: Lynne Gardener, 25 metres back-stroke. She was bound to be prejudiced. All the same . . .

'What do you mean?' he asked cautiously.

Lynne squirmed down until she was lying full-length on the sofa, and started to plait the end of her pony-tail. 'Well, if you were on a ship – ' she began dreamily.

Wait a minute, hold it right there, Andrew thought. 'Why should I be on a ship?' he interrupted. 'I've never been on one up to now. I'll just go on not being on one, thanks very much.'

Lynne stopped plaiting, and thought for a moment. 'Never mind why. Oh, all right then: you're on a ship because we're going on a round-the-world cruise. Mum's been left a lot of money – '

Andrew opened his mouth in disbelief.

' – by a long-lost uncle you've never heard of – '

He shut it again.

' – and we all go on a cruise, OK?' She didn't give Andrew a chance to say that it wasn't. 'One dark night, there's a terrible storm and the ship starts sinking – '

'Ships don't just – '

' – and the captain gives the order *Abandon Ship!*'

Lynne bellowed the order so convincingly that Andrew almost fell off the arm of the sofa.

'They run out the lifeboats, but what

do you think?' Lynne's voice sank to a throaty whisper.

'I think you're making this up,' Andrew said. 'That's what.'

'There isn't enough room in the life-boats for everyone – '

'There's always enough room,' Andrew said, raising his voice. 'There's a law. I wouldn't go on a ship that didn't have enough lifeboats. I'm not stupid.'

His sister looked at him. 'You reckon?' she asked amiably. 'Oh, all right, have it your own way. There *is* enough room on the lifeboats. Every-one climbs in, including you, and they lower the boats into the sea. That's when it happens.' Lynne frowned at the tip of her pony-tail, and bit off a split end. 'Tragic, really.'

'I'm leaving now,' Andrew said. He

went on sitting on the arm of the sofa.

'There's this enormous wave, you see, and one of the lifeboats – '

'Not mine,' Andrew said, trying to

sound confident. 'Not my lifeboat. Was it?' He hadn't meant to let the last bit slip out.

'Actually, yes, I'm afraid it is yours,' Lynne said. 'This absolutely huge wave sweeps down, and the lifeboat carrying you is swamped, and there you are, struggling for your life in the icy water, OK?'

It was a long way from OK in Andrew's opinion, but she didn't wait.

'If you can't swim, what happens then, eh?' she persisted.

Andrew thought fast. He'd learned to do that with Lynne.

'I'd have a life-jacket. So even if my lifeboat was swamped (and I'm not saying it was), I'd be all right. I'd just float around until help came. That's what life-jackets are for, isn't it?'

'Ah, but suppose your life-jacket doesn't work properly. It's got a little, tiny hole in it – '

Andrew wasn't giving in without a fight. 'Even with a little hole, I'd be all right. I'd go on floating for ages.'

'But the hole gets bigger and bigger,' Lynne said calmly, without a trace of sisterly feeling. 'Soon all the air's escaped, and you're out there, in the dark, in the sea, all alone. What do you do then, Andrew, that's what I'd like to know?' She opened her eyes very wide and pointed the tip of the pony-tail at him in a very unfair way. 'Sink or swim?'

Andrew jumped to his feet. 'What *I'd* like to know is what's happened to the rest of you,' he said, aggrieved. 'I mean, there I am, on my own in a sinking lifeboat, with a life-jacket that's got a hole in it, right?'

Lynne nodded.

'Well, where are you and Rob and Mum and Dad while all this is going on? You're supposed to be *looking after* me. Bet your lifeboat doesn't sink. Bet your life-jacket hasn't got holes in. It's always me, every time, who gets the worst of everything!'

Andrew stumped off to his room to put together a model helicopter. He was so annoyed, he put the blades on upside-down. It was quick-setting glue too, so he couldn't take them off again. He went next door to complain to Rob.

Rob was lying on his bed fast asleep. He had exams in the summer, and sleep was his way of building up for them.

'Does it matter?' he said, when Andrew had woken him up and explained about the helicopter. 'It's only a model. It's not as if it's going to fly anywhere.' He shut his eyes again. 'Turn the tape over as you go, would you?'

Andrew stared at him, baffled. 'But it's *wrong*. If a helicopter had blades like that, it would go down, not up. Instead of taking off, it would bury itself in the ground.'

'Congratulations.' Rob rolled over.

'It's the world's first burrowing heli-copter. Think how well it'll go with your hand-held whaling net. Oh, sorry – forgot you gave that to the British Museum. Don't let me keep you, Andrew.'

'You don't *understand*.'

'I don't want to.' Rob put his head under the pillow. 'Goodbye, Andrew,' he said in a muffled voice from under-neath.

Andrew went back to his room. He put the amazing burrowing helicopter on his window-sill. Down below in the garden, his mother was planting some-thing.

Andrew pushed open the window. 'You aren't really going to make me have swimming lessons, Mum, are you?' he called down.

'Yes,' she said. Just like that.

It was enough to make anyone give up.

He shut the window and lay down on the bed to think.

It was all very well for Lynne to go on about him struggling for his life in icy water. She wasn't going to be much better off herself, for all her 25 metres backstroke.

In a raging storm, in the middle of the Atlantic, it wasn't who could swim 25 metres that mattered, anyone could see that. What mattered was who had a working life-jacket. Which, now he came to think about it, Andrew didn't.

Whose stupid idea had it been to take the cruise anyway? Not his, that was certain.

Bet it was Lynne's fault, he thought

bitterly. Bet she nicked my life-jacket too, come to think of it.

Sisters.

Through the bedroom wall came the steady rumble of Rob snoring.

Yeah, that was what was wrong with the world. Sisters, and brothers.

Chapter Two

The next day, Andrew's mother rang the pool.

They said there was space in a children's class at 4.30 on Wednesdays. She put Andrew's name down there and then.

Ten classes. Half an hour a class.

She broke the news when Andrew got home.

'A few lessons, you'll swim like a fish,' she told him.

'I won't,' Andrew answered with quiet determination.

His mother was used to him. 'Try,' she said. 'You never know what you can do till you try.'

So for the next three weeks, Andrew tried.

Mainly he tried to get out of going swimming.

The Tuesday evening before the first lesson, he started coughing.

At breakfast on Wednesday he coughed so hard whenever his mother was within earshot that he hardly had time to eat.

'You're overdoing it,' Lynne said (Rob never came down for breakfast). She moved her cereal out of coughing range.

'Whad d'you beed?' Andrew said carefully. 'I cad't help havig a code.'

'People with colds don't cough, they sniff, you moron. Where's your handkerchief? Why isn't your nose red? Why aren't your eyes watering?'

Andrew gaped at her.

'If you want to get off school, do it properly,' Lynne said impatiently. 'Get it wrong and you'll spoil it for all of us. And if you do . . .'

She had no need to spell out the

consequences. The menace in her voice was enough.

'I don't want to get off school. I just don't want to go – '

'Shut up!' Lynne snapped. 'She's coming!'

Their mother drifted in eating a piece of toast and carrying a mug of

coffee. Trying to make up for lost time, Andrew attempted to cough and sniff simultaneously, overlooking the fact that his mouth was full of cereal.

It was a serious miscalculation.

'Andrew!' his mother cried. 'Are you all right?'

Red-faced, spluttering, eyes streaming, Andrew sneezed a sneeze the like of which he had never sneezed before. 'Got a bit of a code, that's all,' he said bravely when he'd recovered. 'I'll feel better id a day or two.'

'Yes, but I can't send you swimming sounding like that,' his mother said. She dabbed at the coffee stain on her sweater. 'Never mind. I don't expect missing one class will matter.'

One lesson down, nine to go, Andrew calculated.

He was shooting for a perfect record.

A week later, Andrew had a headache Wednesday lunchtime.

The school rang his mother up and she had to take the afternoon off to look after him. The headache was gone by five o'clock – about the same time he ought to have been finishing his swimming lesson.

'Miracle recovery, eh?' His father didn't sound very pleased about it, Andrew thought, holding out his plate for a second helping of pudding.

'Rob used to have miracle recoveries too,' Lynne commented. 'It must run in the family.'

Anyone would think they'd rather he *stayed* ill.

Eight lessons to go.

Andrew was beginning to feel quietly confident.

The Wednesday after that, Andrew couldn't find his swim things.

He called down the stairs to tell his mother.

'They're in your drawer, where they always are,' she called back.

'No, they're not. I've looked there.'

Andrew's mother came up and looked herself.

She looked in the dirty-washing basket, although she knew they wouldn't be there. She looked in the airing cupboard. They weren't there either.

'They must be in here somewhere, love.' She peered round Andrew's room. There wasn't much hope of finding anything smaller than a missing elephant in the mess there.

'Never mind,' Lynne said briskly, sticking her head through the door. 'There's my old two-piece in the airing cupboard. He can use the bottom half of that.'

'Do you think so?' Andrew's mother said doubtfully.

'Of course he can. I don't mind. I'll go and get it.'

The bottom half of Lynne's old swimsuit was pink.

And frilly.

'I can't wear that!' Andrew cried.

'It'll just be for one week,' his mother said comfortably. 'I can't have you missing another lesson. Hurry up, now. We've got to leave for school in five minutes.'

'I'll get you for this,' Andrew told Lynne when their mother had disappeared.

'Who knows,' Lynne answered brightly, 'maybe your own swim things will turn up again. Stranger things have happened.'

She disappeared downstairs, whistling.

'I've found my swim things, Mum,' Andrew said sadly a minute later.

He was going to have to think of something else.

Given the shortage of time available, the best he could come up with was feeling sick an hour before going-home time.

'Funny how it's always on Wednesdays,' his mother said, fetching him from the sick-room. She looked at him thoughtfully. 'Do you want me to ask Darren home to keep you company, love?'

'Yes, please!' Andrew jumped up from the sick-bed.

'Are you well enough, though?' his mother asked.

'Oh yes, I'm much better now,' Andrew said blithely.

His mother nodded. 'Right!' She took him by the arm. 'Let's be off, then.'

'Hey!' Andrew asked as they crossed the junior playground. 'Hadn't I better get Darren?'

'Another time,' his mother said. 'Tonight you're going swimming.'

Chapter Three

The swimming pool was a horrible place.

When Andrew's mother handed over his book of swimming lesson tickets, the girl at the cash desk sniffed. 'He's missed two weeks,' she said, all disapproving.

'He's not been well,' Andrew's mother apologized.

'I'm still not well,' Andrew said loudly.

They ignored him.

'He'll have a lot of catching up to do,' the girl said. She sniffed again. It was obvious that she knew he'd never make a swimmer.

From then on it got worse.

Andrew had to use the girls' changing-room so his mother could come in and show him how to work the lockers. There were girls getting changed there too. He recognized two of them who were from his school, although they were still in the infants. They recognized him too.

It was very embarrassing.

As if that wasn't enough, he knocked his socks off the bench into a suspicious puddle.

'Of course there are puddles on the floor,' his mother said. 'What do you

expect? It's a changing-room. People come in here sopping wet. There's bound to be puddles.'

'I don't like them,' Andrew said truthfully.

The floor tiles felt cold and slimy beneath his feet, and there was a dead handkerchief floating in the water he had to wade through to get to the pool. He didn't like that either.

He would have turned right round and got dressed again if his mother hadn't been standing just behind him, blocking his retreat.

'Go on,' she said cheerfully. 'What are you waiting for? Have fun.'

Andrew gave her a last bitter look and waded gingerly towards his fate.

There were ten children in the lesson: nine would-be swimmers, and Andrew. He stood as far as he could from the others, and tried to look as if they were nothing to do with him. Through a glass panel at the end of the pool he could see his mother making faces at him and waving.

'Go and join the others!' she mouthed through the glass.

Andrew waved coolly back, and stayed right where he was, until Bert, the swimming teacher, came out and told them all to sit on the edge of the pool with their feet in the water.

Even sitting down, Andrew was twice the height of the girl he had to sit next to. She smiled at him too, which was a bit of a cheek in his opinion. *He* didn't go round smiling at complete strangers twice as big as he was.

He smiled back, distantly.

'You *are* thin,' she said, and giggled.

Andrew switched the smile off.

'My name's Gemma. I'm five. I can swim.'

'Bully for you,' Andrew said politely. 'Excuse me. I have to sit somewhere else.' He rose to his feet.

Bert looked up from the list of names he'd been ticking off on his clipboard. 'Hey, you! What's your name? Andrew?

Sit down again, Andrew. Right, all of
you: let's see you kick your feet!'

Andrew sat down again and inserted
one foot cautiously into the water. It
felt peculiar, but not entirely unpleas-
ant. He wriggled his toes.

It was – yes, it was very nearly enjoy-
able.

In a sudden rush of boldness, Andrew lowered his other foot into the water. Maybe swimming wasn't going to be so bad after all. Maybe –

'*That's* not kicking,' Gemma said scornfully. '*This* is kicking.'

She lifted both legs out of the water and – whap! – smacked them down again at speed, one after the other. A great fountain of spray rose into the air and landed on Andrew.

'Great kicking, Gemma!' Bert shouted. 'All right, everyone: no more splashing – into the water.'

Nine children slid off the edge of the pool into the water.

One didn't.

'What's the problem, Andrew?' Bert asked, strolling across.

'Can't we go down the shallow end?'

Andrew pleaded. 'The water's going to be over my knees!'

'This *is* the shallow end,' Bert said. 'Go on, in you go!'

'It was horrible,' Andrew told his mother when the lesson was over. He was huddling in his towel in the changing-room. 'The others are all

littler than me. Two girls splashed me. We had to lie down in the water! We had to jump in!'

'*You* jumped in?' his mother asked hopefully.

Andrew looked at her.

'You didn't jump in,' she said sadly. 'Well, never mind. It'll be better next week, you'll see.'

Andrew knew she was wrong, but he didn't say so. His teeth were chattering too much.

In any case, he'd just noticed a sign on the wall of the changing-room. Maybe there was a way to avoid next week – and the week after, and the week after that.

A spot of research, that was what was called for. And the sooner he got going the better.

Chapter Four

'What's a verruca?' Andrew whispered to Darren next morning while Mr Elliot took the register. He and Darren always sat next to each other, when they were allowed to.

'No talking, Andrew,' Mr Elliot said without looking up.

'A sort of hat,' Darren answered with great confidence. He was confident about everything. It was one of the things Andrew liked about him.

Confident doesn't mean you're *right*, though – at least, not with Darren.

'A hat?' Andrew said doubtfully. 'What sort of hat? Are you sure?'

Silly question really. Of course Darren was sure.

'It's furry,' Darren said knowledge-ably. 'They wear them in Russia. Or Peru. *You* know.'

'No talking, you two.' Mr Elliot still didn't look up.

'Yes, I *know*,' Andrew said quickly. 'But why can't you go swimming if you've got one?'

Darren looked staggered, but only briefly. 'It's something medical. I saw it on the telly. To do with – '

'Darren!' said Mr Elliot loudly.

' – rabies!' Darren finished out of the side of his mouth. 'Here, Mr Elliot!'

Rabies? No wonder they wouldn't let you go swimming if you had one, then. 'Have *you* got a verruca?' Andrew asked next, on the offchance.

'Andrew!' Mr Elliot shouted.

'Here, Mr Elliot!'

'I know you're here, Andrew,' Mr Elliot said more quietly, 'just the way I know Darren is here too. And for once I'm going to do something about it.'

Darren and Andrew spent the rest of the morning on opposite sides of the classroom. When they met up again at break, Darren said he'd once had a verruca but his mum had thrown it out. 'The cat was sick on it,' he said, looking sad.

Andrew was sad too, but not surprised, knowing Darren's cat.

He went round the playground trying to find someone who did have a verruca. Everyone said, 'Ugh, no thank you,' until he came to Helen Pearce.

'Yeah, I've got a verruca. Well, two actually,' Helen said.

Trust Helen to have two of them, Andrew thought.

'I had two once,' Darren said quickly.

Andrew cut in before Darren got on

to the bit about his mum throwing
them away. Break was almost over. He
needed information fast. 'What do they
look like?'

Helen stared at him hard, and then
shrugged. 'I'll show you if you like.' She
sat down on the wall at the edge of the

football field and began to unbuckle one shoe.

'Why are you doing that?' Andrew asked, baffled.

'Because that's where the verrucas are. On my foot,' she explained, surprisingly patient.

'Pull the other one,' Darren said, very man of the world. 'You don't wear hats on your feet.'

'Pull the other one,' Andrew echoed gamely, although by then he had a pretty good idea of what was going to follow.

He was right.

'Too right, I don't wear hats on my feet,' she said in the tone reserved for the sincerely stupid. 'I do have *warts* there, though. That's what a verruca is. It's a special sort of wart. Look.'

She took off her sock. On the bottom of her foot were two small round plasters.

She peeled one off, and underneath was an area about the size of a fruit gum, white and dead-looking, with a substantial crater in the middle. 'That's a verruca.' She stuck the plaster back on, more or less, and pulled on the sock. 'What did you think a verruca was?' she asked.

Luckily the bell rang so they didn't have to answer.

'A furry hat!' Andrew said on the way back to class. 'From Peru! Or was it Moscow?'

'There's more than one sort of verruca,' Darren said with dignity.

Andrew let it pass. At least he only had to fake a wart on his foot, not lash out good pocket money on a furry Peruvian hat. That was something to be thankful for.

Back home, he fished his medical book out of its hiding-place under the bed, and read up on verrucas.

He came down to dinner limping.

'What have you done now?' his mother demanded.

'Dunno,' Andrew said. He'd decided on a subtle approach. Let them work out for themselves what was wrong with him. 'My foot hurts.'

His mother dumped a stack of plates on the table and yelled: 'Lynne! Rob! It's dinner!'

'It's really sore,' Andrew told her. As Lynne and Rob appeared, he hobbled over to the table, wearing the anguished but brave expression he'd spent half an hour practising in front of the bathroom mirror.

Nobody showed the slightest interest.

Lynne sighed as she sat down. 'Baked potatoes *again*?'

Rob said, 'I like baked potatoes,' taking two.

'You would.'

'What's wrong with baked potatoes?' Andrew's father asked, mystified. Lynne launched into a lengthy explanation.

'It's sensitive to pressure,' Andrew said, the first chance he had.

There was a sudden silence. Everyone looked at him.

'Your potato, love?' his mother asked after a moment. She gave her own a doubtful prod. 'Mine's all right. What about yours, Rob?'

'Not my potato, my foot!' Andrew cried before Rob could open his mouth.

They looked at him again.

'What?' his father asked, all at sea.

'Nitrites,' Lynne said in a doom-laden voice.

'It's not nitrites!' Andrew said hotly.

'It's got nothing to do with nitrites, or potatoes.' There was nothing else for it: goodbye the subtle approach, he was going to have to tell them. 'My foot hurts when I walk on it. I think I've got a verruca.'

'Andrew!' his father said. 'Not at dinner.'

His mother looked at him fixedly. 'Have you been at that medical book

again? That one I told you to throw
out?'

Rob and Lynne groaned.

'It's a perfectly good book!' Andrew
said. 'It cost 20p. Why should I throw it
out?'

'It's about a hundred years old,'
Lynne said severely.

'People got ill then too, didn't they?'

'Different illnesses, dear,' his mother

said. 'People don't get bubonic plague nowadays. Poor Darren, no wonder he got all upset. Chicken-pox is bad enough at the best of times without that sort of worry. Now, don't go on about verrucas,' she said, raising her voice. 'I'll have a look at your foot after dinner and see what *is* wrong with it. Until then, I don't want to hear any more about it. Or nitrites.' She gave Lynne a stern look.

The meal finished in silence.

Afterwards Andrew limped off to the sofa for a foot inspection.

'Mmm,' his mother said. 'It hurts when you walk on this foot, right?'

'Yes, right,' Andrew said stiffly. He was still cross about the argument at dinner. Anyone could get bubonic plague mixed up with chicken-pox.

They had a lot in common.

'Then why was it the other foot you were limping on?' his mother asked smartly. 'Really, Andrew, I wasn't born yesterday. That's not a verruca, it's a biro mark. Go up at once and clean it off. And don't bother thinking up any more excuses,' she shouted up the stairs after him. 'Next Wednesday you're going swimming.'

Chapter Five

'Right,' said Bert. 'Everyone go get a float and line up along the rail in the water. I want to see each of you swim across on your back, holding the float. Point your toes, kick hard, and no stopping half-way. You first, Gemma.'

Gemma went all the way across on her back in a storm of splashing. Then the others went, one after another, until it was Andrew's turn.

'Andrew, I said get one float, not six,'

Bert said.

Andrew clutched the floats to his chest. 'I need six. I've got heavy bones. I sink faster.'

'One,' Bert said. 'Go on, put the others back in the pile.'

Andrew put four of the floats back. '*And* the other one,' Bert said, watching closely.

'It's your fault if I drown,' Andrew said as he got back into the water.

'Off you go, Andrew,' Bert told him.

Andrew went right across the pool on his back. Just like that, no trouble.

'There!' Bert said, trying not to sound astonished. 'Told you it was easy. You hardly needed the float at all, I could see that.'

Andrew beamed.

'He had one hand on the bottom all the way,' Gemma said. 'I saw him.'

Bert looked at Andrew and sighed. 'Do it properly next time. Across on your fronts now, everyone.'

They all went across on their fronts, one way or another. Andrew was last as usual. '*Both* hands on the float this time,' Bert warned him as he set off. 'Hold it!' he called a minute later.

'You're only kicking with one foot! What's the other one doing?'

Andrew said nothing.

'His other foot's on the bottom,' Gemma shouted gleefully.

'Take the foot off the bottom and kick it,' Bert said very slowly and clearly. 'Let's go, Andrew.'

Andrew set off once more. When he reached the other side, Bert said, 'Andrew, you were still kicking with one foot. I saw you.'

'It was the other foot,' Andrew said. 'I changed over, just like you told me.'

Bert looked at him for a long time. 'That's all right, then.' He sounded tired. 'For a moment there, I thought you weren't listening to me. All right, everybody: faces in the water and blow bubbles.'

Near the end of the lesson, Bert led them all along to the big pool.

'It's going to be your test in a few weeks,' he told them. 'If you want to pass, you have to jump into deep water. Some of you managed it last week, some of you didn't.' He avoided

looking at Andrew. 'Line up now and let's see how you do this time.'

Andrew went to his usual place at the back of the line. One by one, the children went to the edge of the pool and jumped in. If they were nervous, Bert let them hold his hand before they jumped. Eventually it was Andrew's turn.

'Go on,' Bert said. 'I bet your mum 20p you'd do it today. I need the money. Get closer to the edge – you'd have to be a long-jumper to get in from there. Right, now in you go.'

Nothing happened.

'Can I hold your hand?' Andrew asked.

Bert looked up and down the pool. 'Anyone watching? No? All right, you can hold my hand.'

They stood on the side of the pool holding hands. Andrew peered down into the water.

'Why's it so murky?' he asked. 'I can't see the bottom. There could be anything down there. What if there's fish and stuff? What if there's sharks?'

Bert raised his eyes to the ceiling. 'There's no sharks. Cross my heart,

Andrew, I checked this morning. In you go.'

Bert let go of Andrew's hand, but Andrew didn't let go of Bert's. Bert had to uncurl the fingers one by one. 'Come on, Andrew,' he said firmly. 'Time to jump.'

Andrew looked down into the water. He thought maybe he would jump in. Then he thought maybe he wouldn't. He started to wobble.

He grabbed Bert, but it was too late.

Andrew didn't so much jump into the pool as fall in.

He didn't go alone.

'Great,' Bert said when he surfaced. 'That's 20p your mum owes me. I'm wet but I'm rich. Lesson's over, everyone. Go and get dressed.'

While Andrew dried himself despondently in the changing-room (at least he was allowed to use the boys' one this time), his mother cornered Bert by the floats cupboard.

'He's not getting any better, is he?' she said accusingly.

'Well . . .' Bert tried to think of something positive to say about Andrew's progress, and failed. 'No, he isn't.'

'Isn't there anything else you can do?'

Bert said there wasn't. Where swimming was concerned, Andrew was what might be called a slow learner.

'How slow?' Andrew's mother wanted to know. 'Are we talking weeks or months here? Years?'

Bert didn't say anything. She wondered if he was waiting for her to get on to decades, or centuries. 'How long is it going to take before he can swim?' she insisted.

'It's up to Andrew, really, Mrs Gardener,' Bert said.

She'd been afraid it was something like that.

'When he wants to swim, he'll swim,' Bert went on. 'Surprise us all one day, I bet you.'

'You think so?' Andrew's mother looked a bit more cheerful.

'Stranger things have happened,' Bert said. 'See you next week, Mrs G. Tell you what: why don't you take him swimming yourself at the weekend? That sometimes helps – makes it seem more normal . . . Of course, it's up to you,' he added, seeing her expression.

Mrs Gardener squared her shoulders. 'All right, I'll have a go. If you think it'll do any good, I'll take him swimming this Sunday. We'll all go,' she added grimly. 'It'll be a family outing.'

Chapter Six

First thing on Monday, Mr Elliot always made the class write a page in their diaries about something they'd done at the weekend. He read the paper while they did it, and called out spellings if they were needed.

You could score a lot of points with other members of the class by calling out certain things. Helen Pearce was the expert in this department. 'How do you spell *expensive diamond brace-*

let?' she sang out after the first minute.

Darren nudged Andrew and winked. As soon as Mr Elliot had finished spelling, he raised his hand.

'Yes, Darren?' Mr Elliot looked at him warily.

'How d'you spell *boa constrictor*?'

'Is that a serious question? It had better be.' The week before, Darren had asked how to spell *dynamite*, *gruesome* and *extraterrestrial* only to hand in a perfectly routine description of Sunday lunch at his granny's.

'I went to the zoo,' Darren said in an injured voice. 'I want to write about the reptile house.'

'Of course you do,' Mr Elliot said with a sigh. He spelled out *boa constrictor* for Darren, *sapphire* for Helen, and then *alligator*, *pearl earrings*,

python and *sequinned*, in quick succession, before putting his head down on the desk and covering it with his newspaper.

Andrew put his hand up. 'How do you spell *casualty*, please? Oh, and how many Ss are there in *concussion*?'

Darren looked at him with surprise and admiration.

'I've had enough, Andrew,' Mr Elliot said without moving.

'But I need lots more,' Andrew protested. 'I need *resuscitation*, and *ambulance*, and *emergency*, and all sorts of things. I've never had to use them before. It's the first time we've all gone swimming,' he pleaded.

'Andrew,' Mr Elliot spoke from under the paper, 'this week's competition is officially closed. I hereby declare Darren the winner from Helen by one sequinned python, and if I get any more improbable requests from anybody, *they'll* be the ones in need of resuscitation.' He removed the newspaper from his head and looked round the classroom. 'Do I make myself clear?'

'Yes, Mr Elliot,' everybody said.

Andrew had to find a way round the spellings, but he didn't really mind.

Mr Elliot obviously didn't mind either. Once he'd read the diary himself, he apologized to Andrew and asked him to read it out loud to the whole class. So Andrew stood up at the front and read:

We went swimming on Sunday. Nobody wanted to, but Mum said we had to. So we did.

Lynne said she'd show me backstroke but she bumped into a lifeguard and knocked him out. They asked her to leave the pool. She said she was never going to come again. (*Good!* the lifeguard shouted as she left.)

Mum stubbed her toe jumping in. She spent the whole time in the first-aid room with Bert, watching snooker on television.

Rob tried to do a racing turn but he hates opening his eyes under water. He kept them shut and hit the wall nose first.

When Dad saw all the blood in the water, he fainted. The ambulance came and took both of them off to casualty.

Mum and I had an ice cream with Bert to celebrate, and then we went home.

Mr Elliot put up his hand. 'Thank you very much, Andrew. One thing, though: what was it you were celebrating, if you don't mind my asking?'

Andrew blinked. 'Didn't I put that bit in? While everyone else was down the other end of the pool watching the ambulance men look after Rob and Dad, I had the little pool all to myself. First I sort of took one foot off the bottom and did this.' Andrew waved his right arm in a complicated fashion.

'And then I took the other foot off and did that.' He waved his left arm instead. 'And then I sort of took both feet off together, and did this.' Andrew beat the air violently with both arms at once, and made a terrible face. 'And . . . I didn't sink!' he said, still astonished at the memory. 'I did five whole kicks, no float, no foot on the bottom, nothing.'

'You mean . . . ?' asked Mr Elliot.

'Yes!' Andrew shouted. 'I can swim!'